FAVORITE MOTHER GOOSE RHYMES

Little Miss Muffet

Published in the United States of America by The Child's World®
1980 Lookout Drive • Mankato, MN 56003-1705
800-599-READ • www.childsworld.com

Acknowledgments
The Child's World®: Mary Berendes, Publishing Director
Editorial Directions: E. Russell Primm, Editor; Lucia Raatma, Proofreader
The Design Lab: Kathleen Petelinsek, Art Direction and Design;
   Anna Petelinsek and Victoria Stanley, Page Production

Library of Congress Cataloging-in-Publication Data
Jacobs, Joni.
  Little Miss Muffet / illustrated by Joni Jacobs.
       p. cm. — (Favorite Mother Goose rhymes)
  Summary: Presents the classic nursery rhyme about a girl and a spider.
  ISBN 978-1-60253-304-2 (library bound : alk. paper)
  1. Nursery rhymes. 2. Children's poetry. [1. Nursery rhymes.]
I. Mother Goose. II. Title. III. Series.
  PZ8.3.J1374Li 2009
  398.8—dc22   2009001564

ILLUSTRATED BY JONI JACOBS

Little Miss Muffet
sat on a tuffet . . .

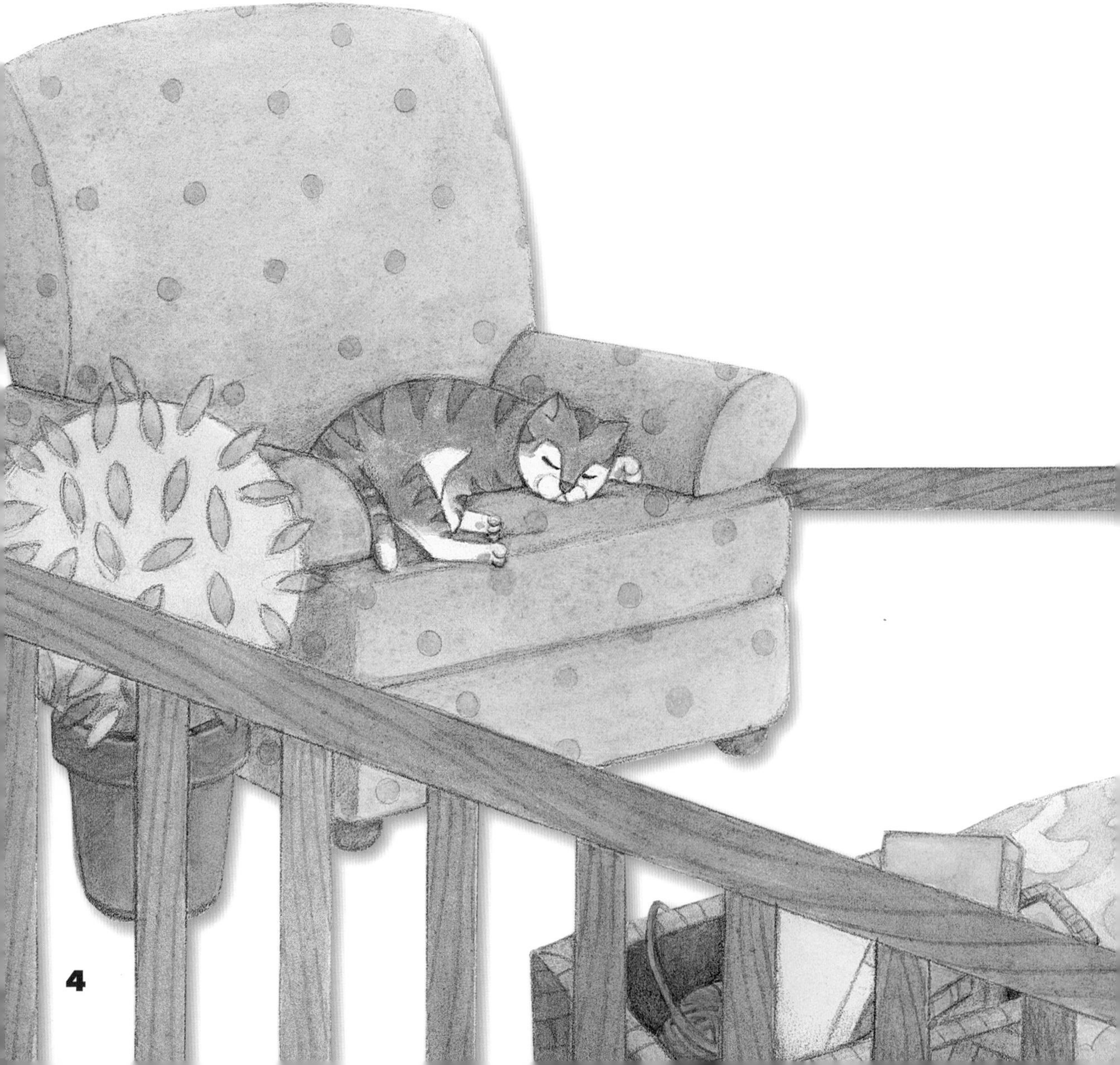

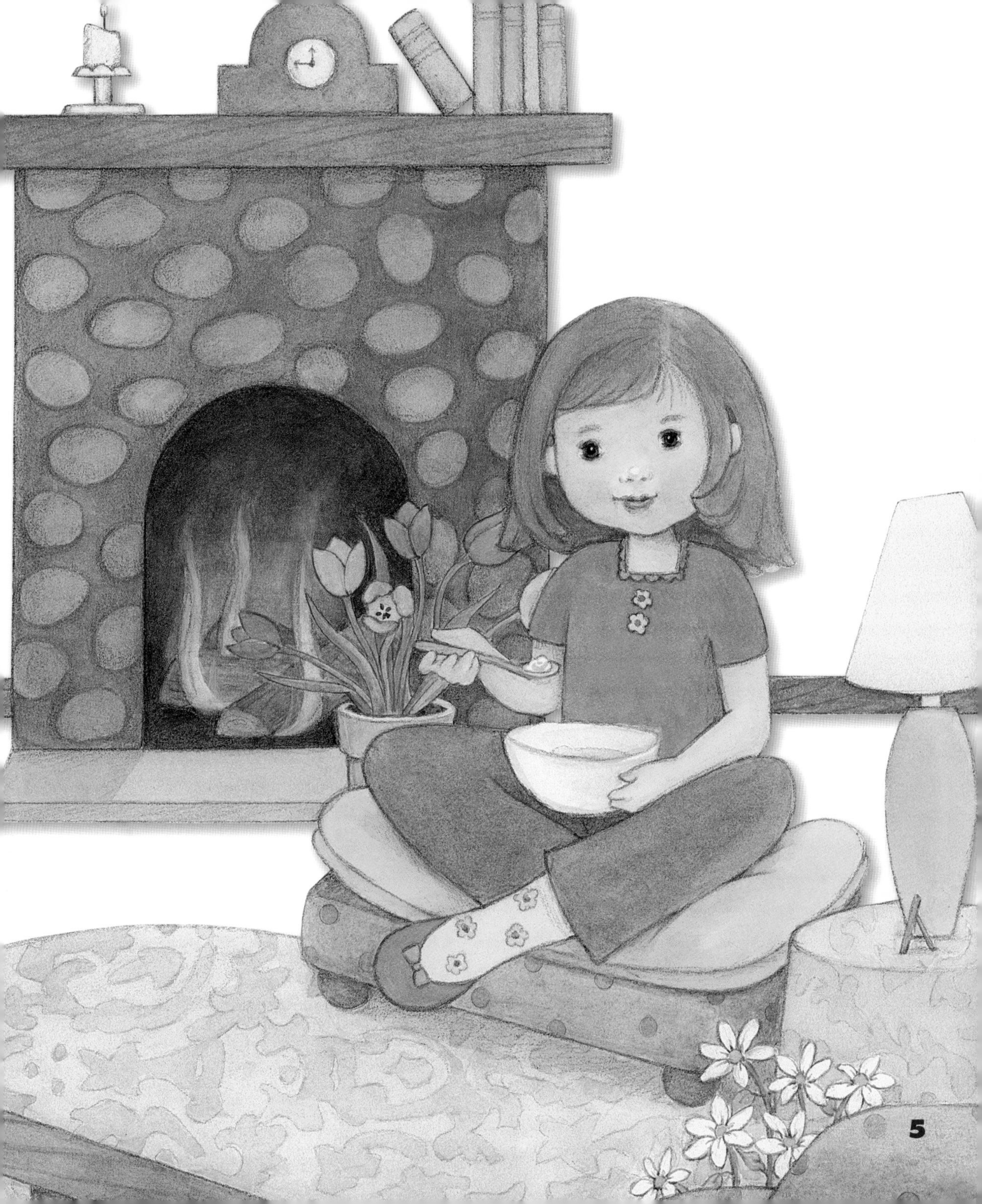

. . . eating her curds
and whey.

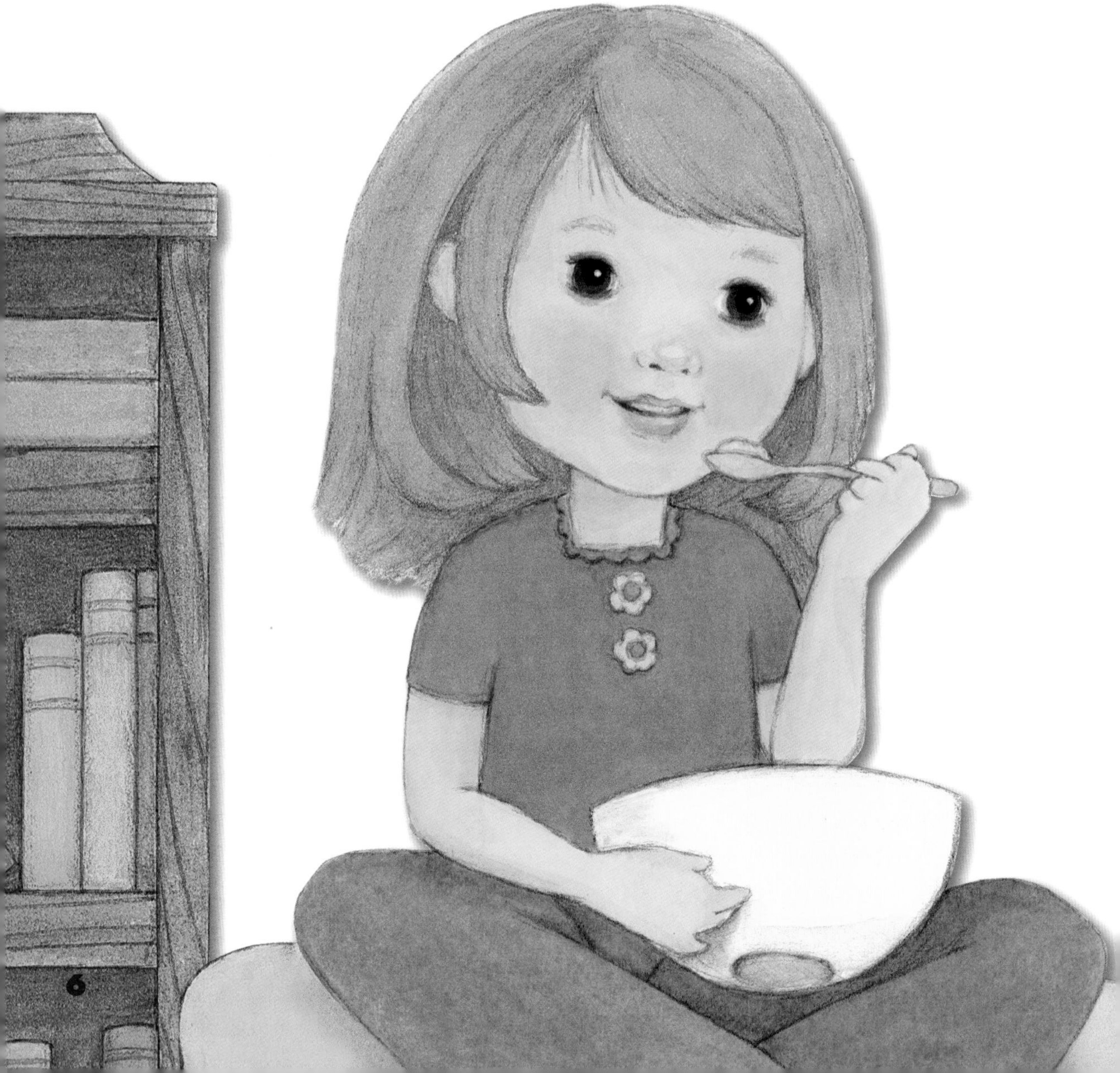

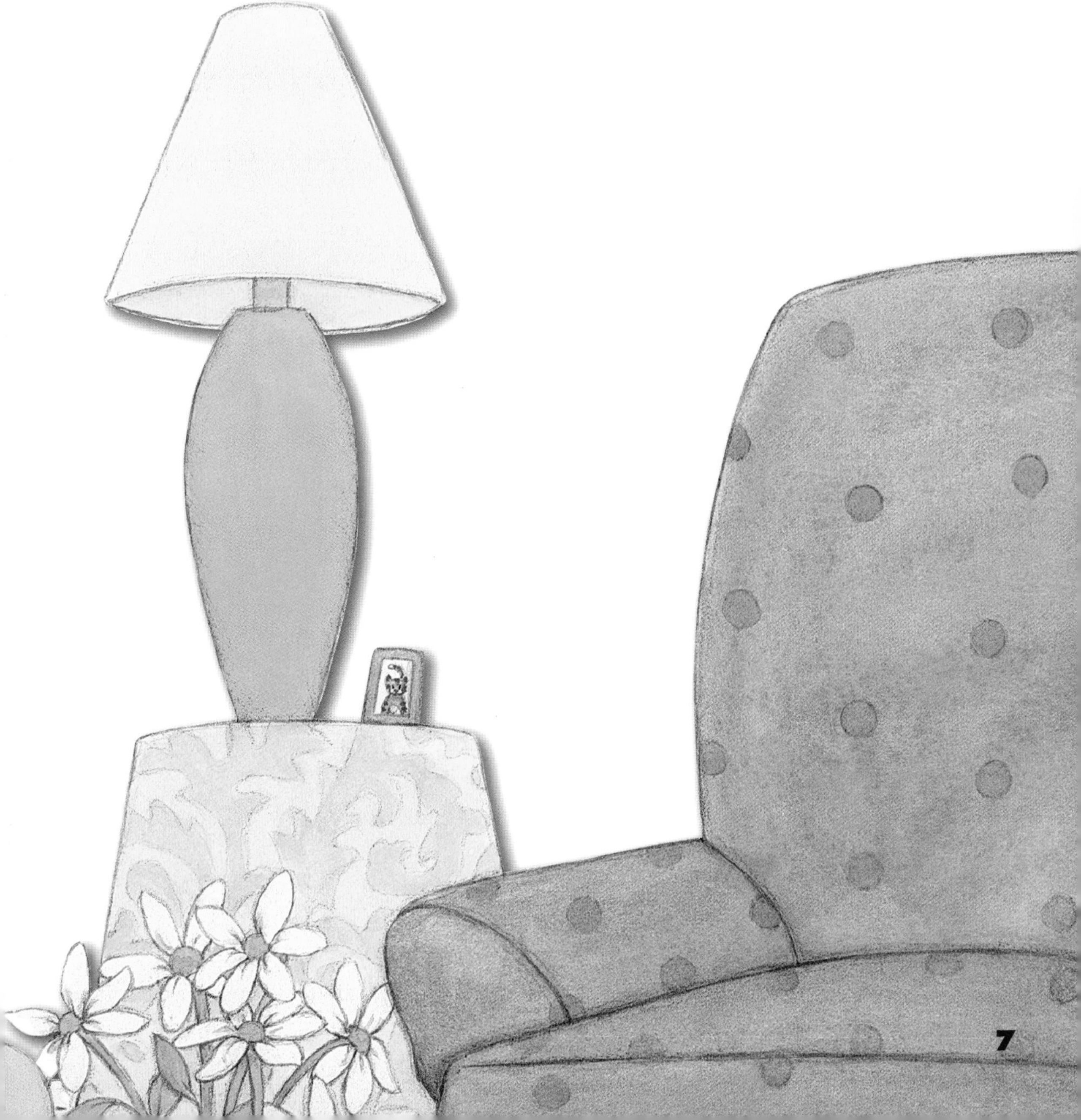

Along came a spider . . .

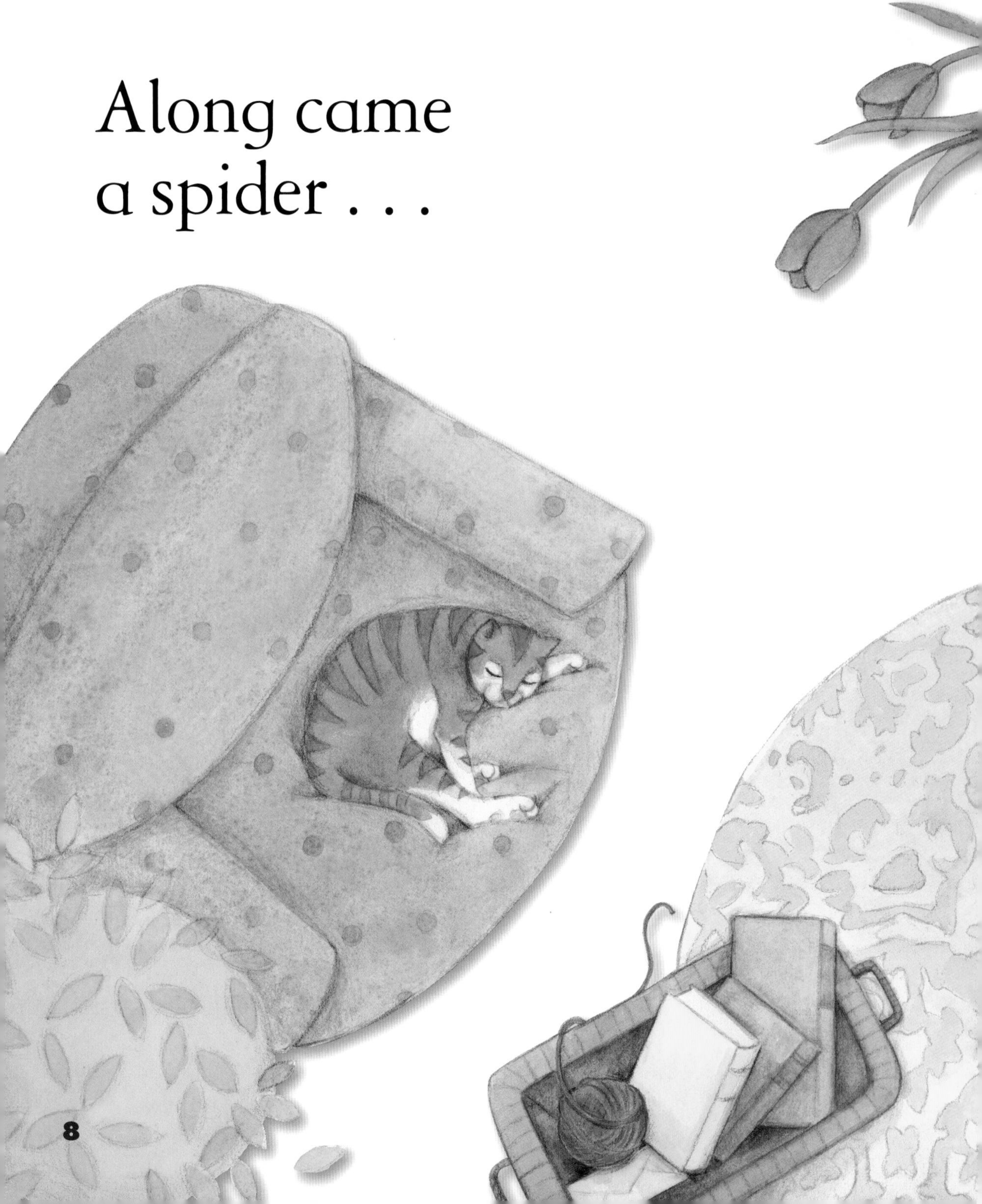

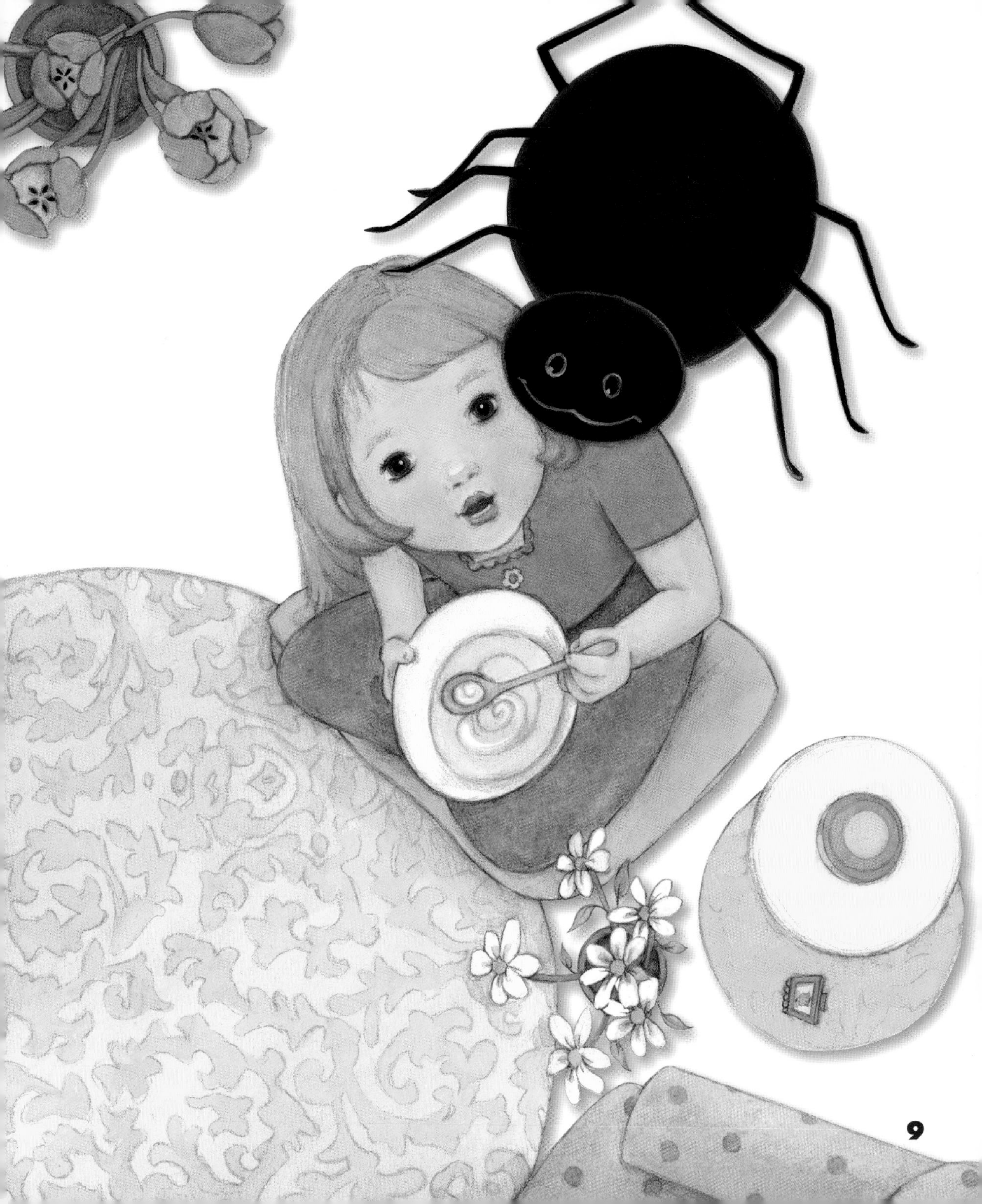

. . . who sat down
beside her . . .

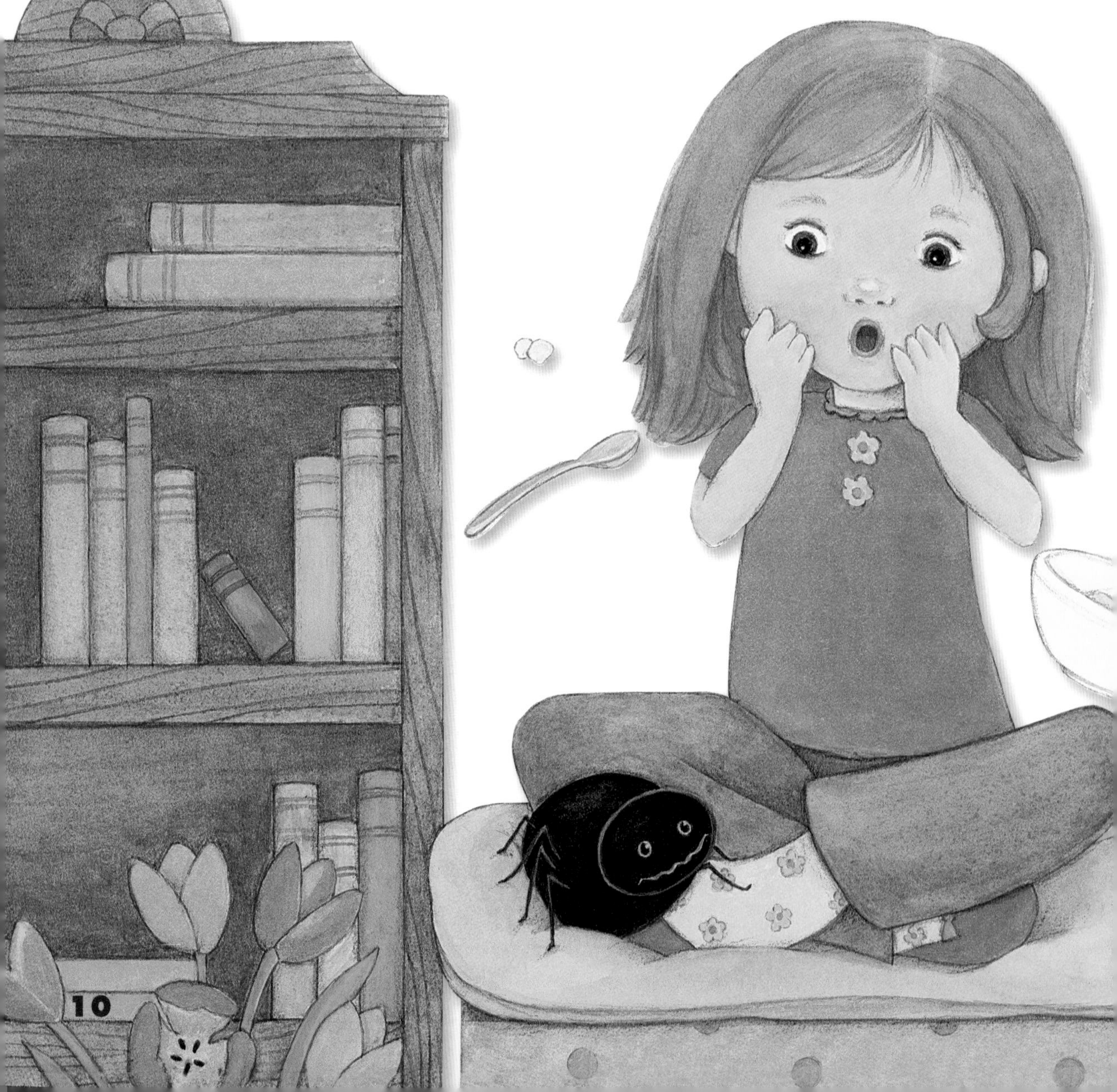

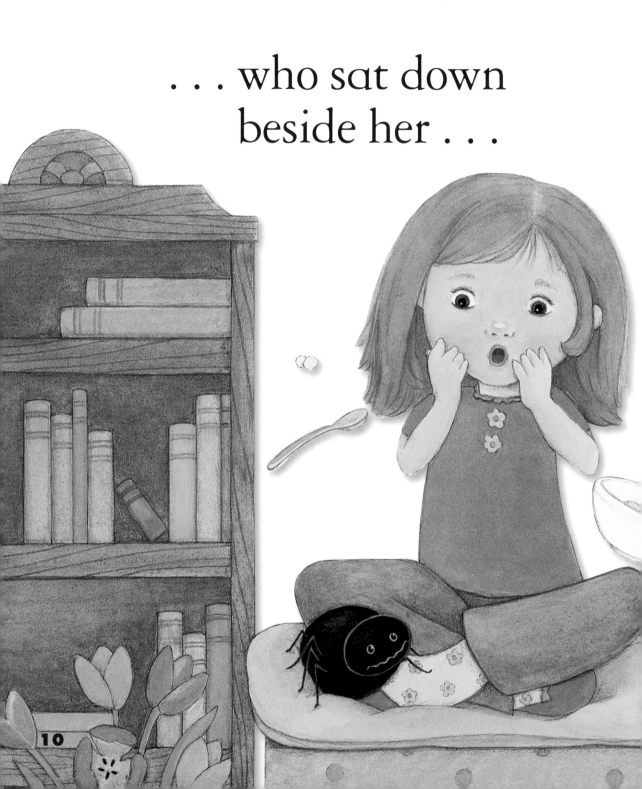

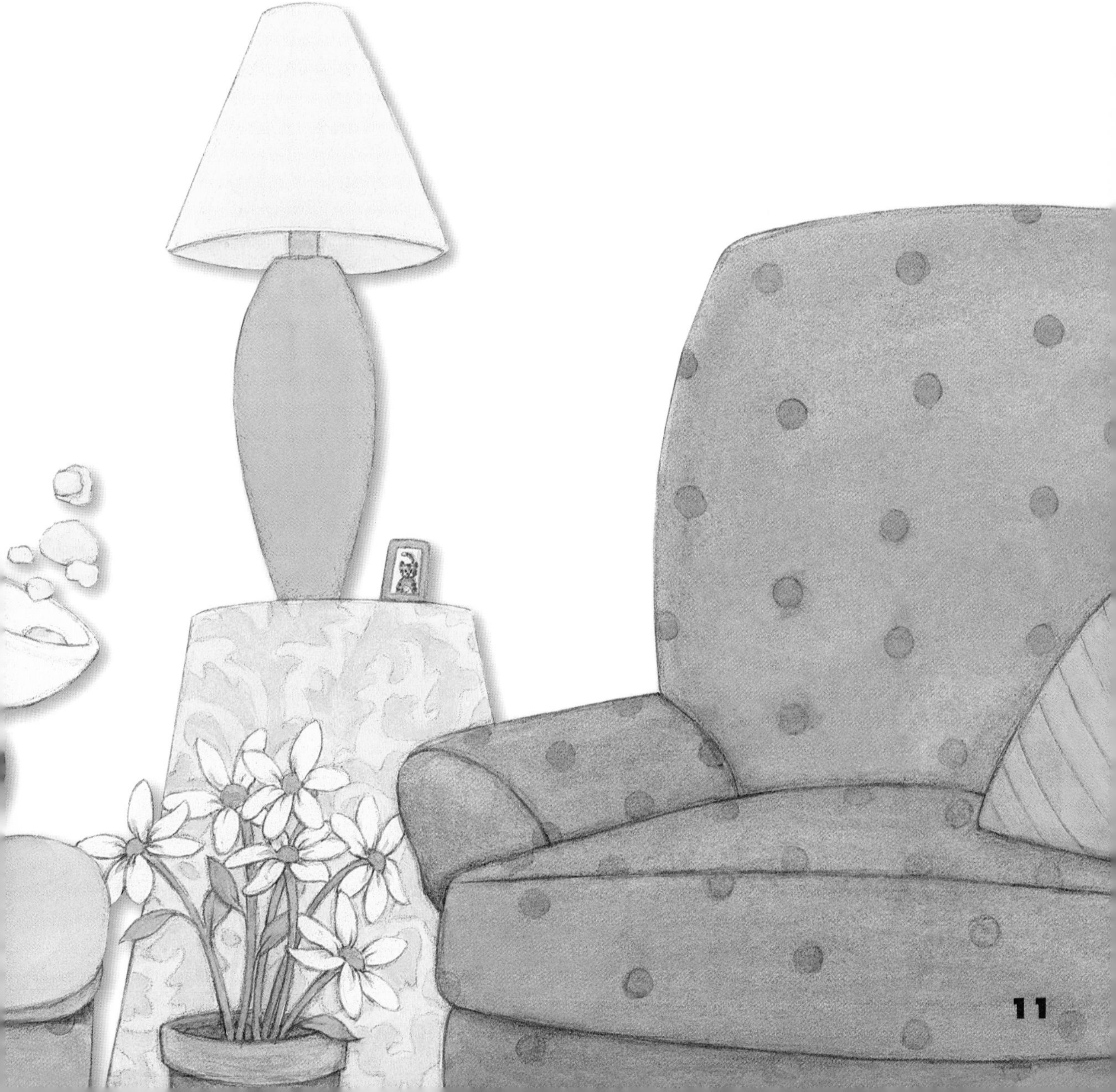

. . . and frightened Miss Muffet away.

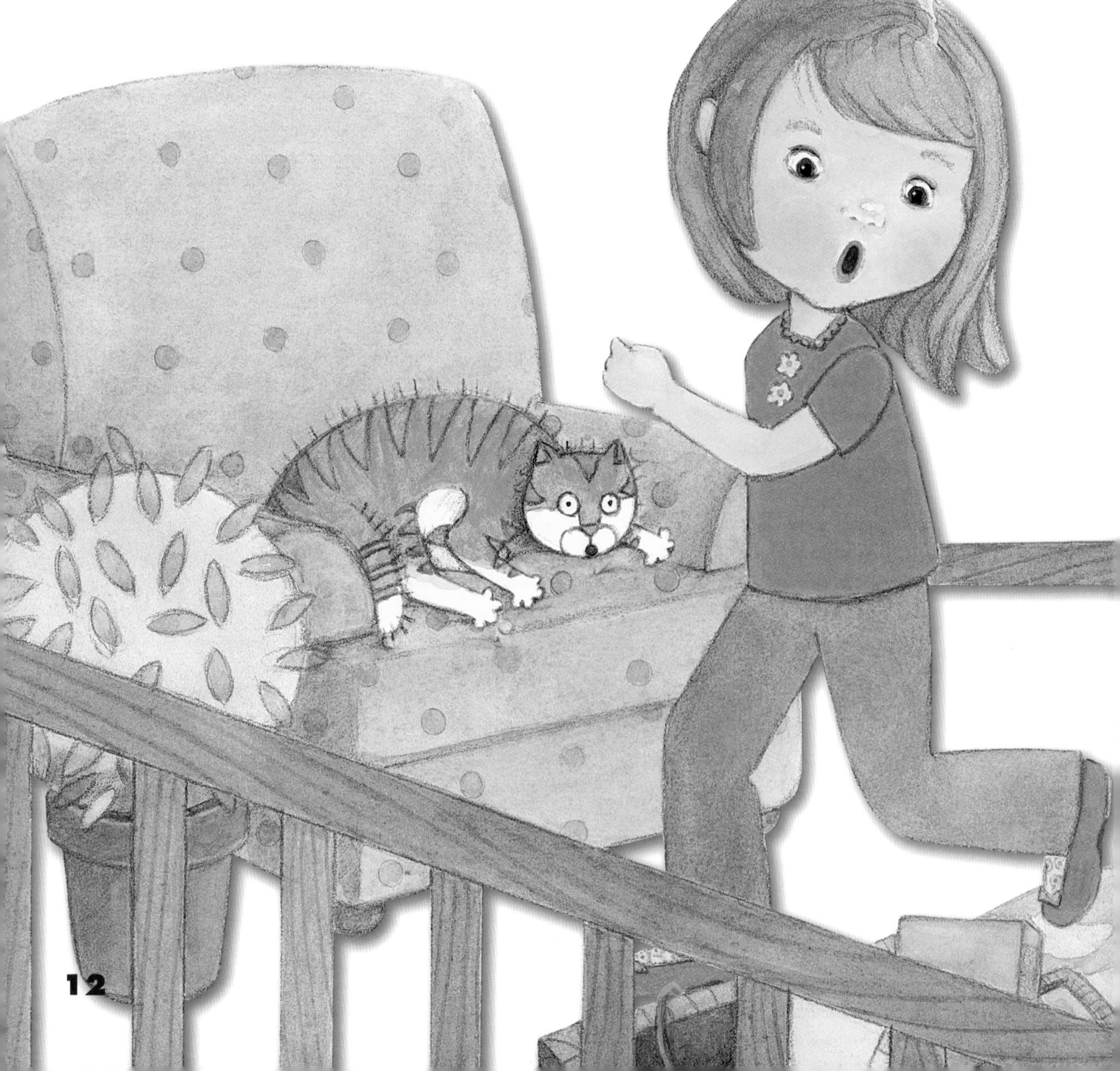

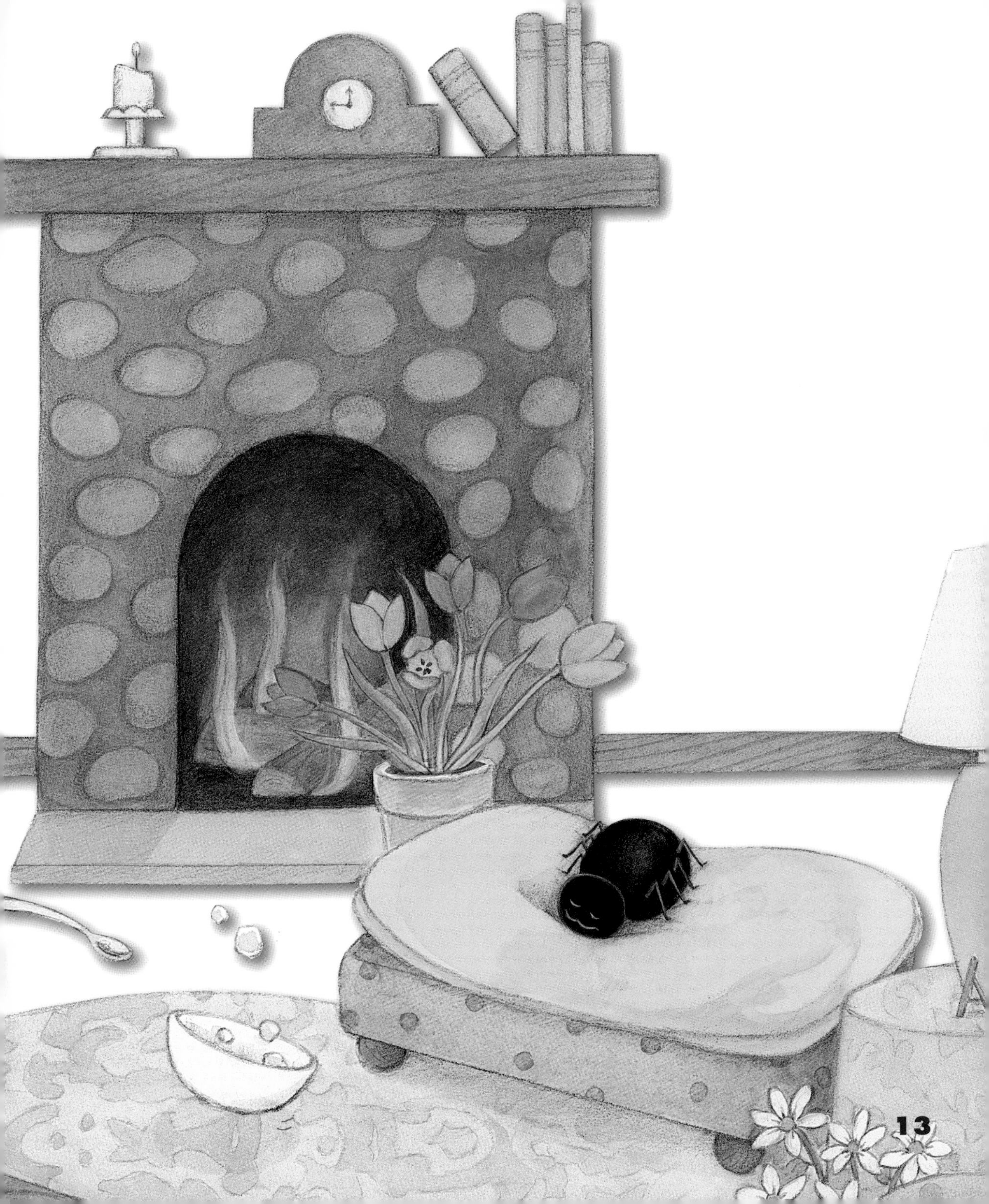

ABOUT MOTHER GOOSE

We all remember the Mother Goose nursery rhymes we learned as children. But who was Mother Goose, anyway? Did she even exist? The answer is . . . we don't know! Many different tales surround this famous name.

Some people think she might be based on Goose-footed Bertha, a kindly old woman in French legend who told stories to children. The inspiration for this legend might have been Queen Bertha of France, who died in 783 and whose son Charlemagne ruled much of Europe. Queen Bertha was called Big-footed Bertha or Queen Goosefoot because one foot was larger than the other.

The name "Mother Goose" first appeared in Charles Perrault's *Les Contes de ma Mère l'Oye* ("Tales of My Mother Goose"), published in France in 1697. This was a collection of fairy tales including "Cinderella" and "Sleeping Beauty"—but these were stories, not poems. The first published Mother Goose nursery rhymes appeared in England in 1781, as *Mother Goose's Melody; or Sonnets for the Cradle*. But some of the verses themselves are hundreds of years old, passed along by word of mouth.

Although we don't really know the origins of Mother Goose or her nursery rhymes, we *do* know that these timeless verses are beloved by children everywhere!

ABOUT THE ILLUSTRATOR

Joni Jacobs graduated from the Art Institute of Pittsburgh in 1983. She has been creating art ever since. Joni currently lives in Northfield, Minnesota. Who needs hands when you have eight legs . . . there is no artist like a spider!

DATE DUE

OCT 2 5 2010		

Demco, Inc. 38-293